Sémiramis

Voltaire

Translation by William F. Fleming

Start Publishing PD LLC
Copyright © 2024 by Start Publishing PD LLC

Start Publishing PD is a registered trademark of Start Publishing PD LLC
Manufactured in the United States of America

Cover art: Shutterstock/Taisiya Kozorez

Cover design: Jennifer Do

10 9 8 7 6 5 4 3 2 1

ISBN 979-8-8809-1130-1

Contents

Dramatis Personæ

Sémiramis.

Arsaces, or Ninias.

Azema, a Princess of the Family of Belus.

Assur, a Prince of the Family of Belus.

Oroes, High Priest.

Otanes, a Favorite of Semiramis.

Mitranes, Friend of Arsaces.

Cedar, Friend of Assur. Guards, Magi, Slaves, Attendants.

This was produced in 1748 and a burlesque upon it was played at Fontainebleau.

ACT I.

The scene represents a large peristyle, at the bottom of which is the palace of Sémiramis. Gardens with fine hanging terraces, raised above the palace: on the right hand the temple of the magi, and on the left a mausoleum adorned with obelisks.

SCENE I.

Arsaces, Mitranes.

[Two slaves at a distance carrying a coffer.]

Arsaces: Once more, Mitranes, thou beholdest thy friend, Who, in obedience to the royal mandate In secret sent, revisits Babylon, The seat of empire; how Sémiramis Imprints the image of her own great soul On every object! these stupendous piles, These deep enclosures, where Euphrates pours His tributary waves; the temple's pride, The hanging gardens, and the splendid tomb Of Ninus, wondrous monuments of art! And only less to be admired than she Who raised them! here, in all her splendid pomp, More honored than the monarchs of the East, Arsaces shall behold this glorious queen.

Mitranes: O my Arsaces, credit not the voice Of Fame, she is deceitful oft, and vain; Perhaps hereafter thou mayest weep with me, And admiration on a nearer view May turn to pity.

Arsaces: Wherefore?

Mitranes: Sunk in grief, Sémiramis hath spread o'er every heart The sorrows which she feels; sometimes she raves, Filling the air with her distressful cries, As if some vengeful God pursued her; sits Silent and sad within these lonely vaults, Sacred to night, to sorrow, and to death, Which mortals dare not enter; where the ashes Of Ninus, our late honored sovereign, lie: There will she oft fall on her knees and weep: With slow and fearful steps she glides along, And beats her breast besprinkled with her tears: Oft as she treads her solitary round, Will she repeat the names of son and husband, And call on heaven, which in its anger seems To thwart her in the zenith of her glory.

Arsaces: Whence can her sorrow flow?

Mitranes: The effect is dreadful: The cause unknown.

Arsaces: How long hath she been thus Oppressed, Mitranes?

Mitranes: From the very time When first her orders came to bring **Arsaces:** Arsaces: Me, saidst thou?

Mitranes: You, my lord: when Babylon Rejoicing met to celebrate thy conquests, And saw the banners thy victorious arm Had wrested from our vanquished foes; when first Euphrates brought to our delighted shore The lovely Azema, from Belus sprung, Whom thou hadst saved from Scythian ravishers, Even in that hour of triumph and success, Even in the bosom of prosperity, The heart of majesty was pierced with grief, And the throne lost its lustre.

Arsaces: Azema Was not to blame; she could not be the cause Of sorrow or distress; one look from her Would soothe the wrath of gods: but say, my friend, Sémiramis is still a sovereign here, Her heart is not forever sunk in grief?

Mitranes: No: when her noble mind shakes off the burden, Resumes its strength, and shines in native lustre, Then we behold in her exalted soul Powers that excel whatever flattery's self Hath e'er bestowed on kings; but when she sinks Beneath this dreadful malady, loose flow The reins of empire, dropping from her hand; Then the proud satrap, fiery Assur, guides The helm and makes the nations groan beneath him: The fatal secret never yet hath reached The walls of Babylon: abroad we still Are envied, but, alas! we mourn at home.

Arsaces: What lessons of instruction to weak mortals, When happiness is mingled thus with woe! I, too, am wretched, thus deprived of him Whose piercing wisdom best could give me council, And lead me through the mazes of a court. O I have cause to weep: without a father, Left as I am to all the dangerous passions Of heedless youth, without a friendly guide, What rocks encompass and what shoals affright me!

Mitranes: I weep with thee the loss of him we loved, The good old man; Phradates was my friend; Ninus esteemed and gave to him the care Of Ninias, his dear son, our country's hope: But O! one fatal day destroyed them both, Father and son: to voluntary exile Devoted, long he lived: his banishment Was fortunate to thee, and made thee great: Close by his side, in honor's glorious field, Arsaces fought, and conquered for his country: Now, ranked with princes, thy exalted virtue Claims its reward by merit all thy own.

Arsaces: I know not what may be my portion here: Perhaps, distinguished on Arbazan's plains With fair success, my name is not unknown: On Oxus' banks to great Sémiramis, When vanquished nations paid the homage due, From her triumphant cars she dropped a ray Of her own glory on Arsaces' head: But oft the soldier, honored in the field, In courts neglected lies, and is forgotten. My father told me in his dying hour The fortune of Arsaces here depended Upon the common cause; then gave to me These precious relics, which from every eye He had preserved: I must deliver them To the high priest, for he alone can judge, And know their value: I must talk with him In secret, touching my own fate, for he Can best conduct me to Sémiramis.

Mitranes: He seldom sees the queen: in solitude Obscure he lives: his holy ministry Engrosses all his care; without ambition, Fearless, and void of art: is always seen Within the temple, never at the court: Never affects the pride of rank and title, Nor his tiara near the diadem Immodest wears: the less he seeks for greatness, The more is he admired, the more revered: I have access to every avenue Of his retirement in this sacred place, And can this moment talk to him in secret; Ere day's too far advanced I'll bring him hither.

SCENE II.

Arsaces: [Alone.] Immortal gods! for what am I reserved? Make known your will: why did my dying father Thus send me to the sanctuary, me A soldier, bred amidst the din of arms? A lover, too? How can Arsaces serve The gods of the Chaldæans?—Ha! what voice From yonder tomb in plaintive accents strikes My frighted ear, and makes my hair to stand On end with horror! Near this place I've heard The spirit of Ninus dwells—again it shrieks— It shocks my soul—Ye dark and dreary caves, And thou, the shade of my illustrious master, Thou voice of heaven, what wouldst thou with Arsaces?

SCENE III.

Arsaces, Oroes, the High Priest, the Magi Attending Him, Mitranes.

Mitranes: [Speaking to Oroes.] He's here, my lord, and waits to give you up Those precious relics.

Arsaces: Most revered father, Permit a soldier to approach your presence, Pleased to fulfil a father's last command, One whom you deigned to love; thus at your feet, Obedient to his will, I here resign them.

Oroes: Welcome! thou brave and noble youth! that God Who governs all, and not a father's will, Guided thee here: Phradates was my friend; Dear is his memory to me; thou shalt know Perhaps hereafter how I love his son: Where are the gifts he sent me?

Arsaces: [The slaves deliver the coffer to two of the magi, who place it on an altar.]

Here, my lord.

Oroes: [Opening the coffer, bowing reverentially to it, and seeming greatly affected.]

Ye sacred relics! do these eyes at length Behold you! O, I weep for joy to press These monuments of woe, whilst tears recall My solemn oath: Mitranes, let no ear Profane disturb our holy mystery: We would be private. [The magi retire.] Mark this seal, Arsaces: 'Tis that which to the laws of Ninus gave Their public force, and kept the world in awe: The letter, too, which with his dying hand He wrote: Arsaces, view the wreath that crowned His royal brows, and his victorious sword: The vanquished Medes and Persians felt its power: It comes at last to vindicate its master, And to revenge him; useless instrument Against base treachery, and destructive poison, Whose mortal—

Arsaces: Heaven! what sayest thou?

Oroes: The dread secret Hath long been hid in darkness from the eyes Of men within the sepulchre; the shade Of Ninus, and offended heaven, long time Have raised their voice in vain, and called for vengeance.

Arsaces: It must be as thou sayest: for know, but now, Even on this spot, I heard most dreadful groans.

Oroes: It was the voice of Ninus.

Arsaces: Twice the noise Affrighted me.

Oroes: 'Twas he: he calls for vengeance.

Arsaces: He has a right to ask it: but on whom?

Oroes: On the vile murderers, whose detested hands Had of the best of sovereigns robbed mankind; No tracks are left behind of the base treason, But all with him lies buried in the tomb: With ease might they deceive the sons of men, But not the all-seeing eye of watchful heaven, Which pierces the deep night of human falsehood.

Arsaces: O would to heaven this feeble hand had power To punish crimes like these! I know not wherefore, But when I cast my eyes towards you tomb, New horrors rise: O might I not consult That venerable shade, the inhabitant Of those dark mansions?

Oroes: No; it is forbidden: An oracle severe long since denounced The wrath of heaven against whoe'er should press Into this vale of tears, inhabited By death and the avenging gods: await With me, Arsaces, for the day of justice: Soon will it come, and all shall be accomplished: I can no more: sequestered from the world, I pray in secret to offended heaven, Which, as it wills, commissions me to speak, Or close my lips in silence: I have said All that I dare, and all I ought: be careful Lest in these walls a word, or look, or gesture, Betray the secret which the god by me Hath trusted with thee; for on that depends His glory, Asia's welfare, and thy life. Approach, ye magi, hide these sacred relics Beneath the altar. [The great gate of the palace opens, Assur appears at a distance, surrounded by attendants and guards on every side.] Ha! the palace opens: The courtiers crowding to the queen: behold The haughty Assur with his servile throng Of flatterers round him! O almighty power! On whom dost thou bestow thy bounties here? O monster!

Arsaces: Ha! what meanest thou?

Oroes: Fare thee well: When night shall cast her sable mantle o'er These guilty walls, I'll have more converse with thee, Before the gods: revere them, my Arsaces, For know, brave youth, their eyes are fixed on thee.

SCENE IV.

Arsaces, Mitranes, in the front of the stage, Assur, Cedar, with attendants, on one side.

Arsaces: His words are dreadful; they affright my soul: What horrid crimes! and what a court is here! How little known! my royal master poisoned, And Assur, but too well I see, suspected!

Mitranes: Assur is sprung of royal race, and claims The deference due to his authority: He is the favorite of Sémiramis, And thou, without a blush, mayest pay him homage.

Arsaces: Homage to him!

Assur: [To Cedar.] Ha! do my eyes deceive me, Or is Arsaces here without my order? Amazing insolence!

Arsaces: What haughtiness!

Assur: [Advancing.] Come hither, youth: what new engagements here Have brought you from the camp?

Arsaces: My duty, sir, And the queen's orders.

Assur: Did the queen send for you?

Arsaces: She did.

Assur: But, know you not, with her commands You should have asked for mine?

Arsaces: I know not that, And should have thought the honor of her crown Debased by such a mean submission to thee: My lord, you must forgive a soldier's roughness, We are bad courtiers: bred up in the plains Of Arbazan and Scythia, I have served Your court, but am not much acquainted with it.

Assur: Age, time, and place, perhaps, may teach you, sir. What would you with the queen? for know, young man, Assur alone can lead you to her presence.

Arsaces: I come to ask my valor's best reward, The honor still to serve her.

Assur: Thou wantest more, Presumptuous boy! I know thy bold pretences To Azema, but that thou wouldst conceal.

Arsaces: Yes: I adore that lovely maid: her heart Would I prefer to empire: my respect, My tenderest love—

Assur: No more: thou knowest not whom Thou art insulting thus: what! join the race Of a Sarmatian to the demigods Of Tigris and Euphrates! mark me well: In pity to thy youth I would advise thee Ne'er, on thy peril, to Sémiramis Impart thy insolent request; for know, Rash boy, if thou shouldst dare to violate The rights of Assur, 'twill not pass unpunished.

Arsaces: I'll go this instant: thou hast given me courage: Thus threatenings always terrify Arsaces: Thou hast no right, whate'er thy power may be, To affront a soldier who has served his queen, The state, and thee: perhaps my warmth offends; But thou art rasher than myself, to think That I would bend beneath thy servile yoke, Or tremble at thy power.

Assur: Perhaps thou mayest; I'll teach thee what a subject may expect For insolence like this.

Arsaces: We both may learn it.

SCENE V.

Sémiramis, at the farther end of the stage, leaning on her women.

Otanes, Assur, Arsaces, Mitranes, in the Front.

Otanes: [Advancing.] My lord, the queen at present would be private: You must retire, and give her sorrows way: Withdraw, ye gods, the hand of vengeance from her!

Arsaces: How I lament her fate!

Assur: [To one of his attendants.] Let us begone, And study how we best may turn her griefs To our advantage. [Sémiramis comes forward, and is joined by **Otanes: Otanes:** My royal mistress, be yourself again, And wake once more to joy and happiness.]

Sémiramis: O death! when wilt thou come with friendly shade To close these eyes that hate the light of day? Be shut, ye caves; horrible phantom, hence! Strike if thou wilt, but threaten me no more. Otanes, is Arsaces come?

Otanes: Ere morn Rose on the temple, madam, he was there.

Sémiramis: That dreadful voice, from heaven or hell I know not, Which in the dead of night so shakes my soul, Told me, my sorrows, when Arsaces came, Would soon be o'er.

Otanes: Rely then on the gods, And let the cheerful ray of hope dispel This melancholy.

Sémiramis: Is Arsaces here? Methinks, when I but hear his name, my soul Is less disturbed, and guilt sits lighter on me!

Otanes: O! quit, forever quit the sad remembrance: Let the bright days of great Sémiramis, Replete with glory, blot one moment out That broke the chain of thy ill-fated nuptials: Had Ninus driven thee from his throne and bed, All Babylon with thee had been destroyed; But happily for us, and for mankind, That wanted such distinguished virtues, you Prevented him; and fifteen years of toil, Spent in the service of thy country, lands Desert and waste made fertile by thy care, The savage tamed, and yielding to the laws, The useful arts, obedient to thy voice, Uprising still, the glorious monuments Of wealth and power, the wonder of mankind, And the loud plaudit of a grateful people, All plead thy cause before the throne of heaven; But if impartial justice hold the scale, If vengeance is required for Ninus' death, Why thus should Assur brave the angry gods, And live in peace? He was more guilty far Than thou wert, yet the ruthless hand that poured The fatal draught never shakes with fear: he feels No stings of conscience, no remorse affrights him.

Sémiramis: Our duties different, different is our fate: Where ties are sacred, crimes are heavier far: I was his wife, Otanes, and I stand Without excuse; my conscience is my judge And my accuser: but I hoped the gods, Offended at my crimes, had punished me Enough, when they deprived me of my child; Hoped my successful toils, that made the earth Respect my name, had soothed the wrath of heaven: But months on months have passed in agony Since this dire spectre hath appalled my soul: My eyes forever see him, and my ears Still hear his cries: I get me to the tomb, But dare not enter: trembling I revere His ashes, and invoke his honored shade, Which only answers me in dismal groans. Some dread event is nigh: perhaps the time Is come to expiate the offence.

Otanes: But thinkest thou The spirit of thy lord hath left indeed The mansions of the dead, and stalks abroad? Ofttimes the soul, by powerful fancy led, Starts at a phantom of its own creation; Still it beholds the objects it has made, And everything we fear is present to us.

Sémiramis: O no! it was not the wild dream of fancy By slumber wrought, I saw him but too well: The stranger, Sleep, had long withheld from me His sweet delusions; watchful as I stood, And mused on my unhappy fate, a voice Close to my bed, methought, cried out, "Arsaces!" The name revived me: well thou knowest, long time Assur has pierced this heart with deadly grief: I shudder at his presence, and the blushes That show my guilt increase my punishment, Hate the reproachful witness of my shame, And wish I could—but wherefore should I add To crimes like mine fresh guilt? I sought Arsaces To punish Assur, and the thought of him Awhile relieved me! but in the sweet moment Of consolation, sudden stood before me That minister of death, all bathed in blood, And in his hand a falchion: still I see, Still hear him: comes he to defend, or punish? 'Twas at that very hour Arsaces came. This day was fixed by heaven to end my sorrows, But peace is yet a stranger to my soul, And hope is lost in horror and despair: The load of life is grown too heavy for me, My throne is hateful, and my glories past But add fresh weight to my calamities. Long time I've hid my sorrows from the world And blushed in secret, fearful to consult That reverend sage whom Babylon adores: I would not thus degrade the majesty Of sovereign power, or let Sémiramis Betray her fears before a mortal's eye, But I have sent to Libya's sands in secret There to consult the oracle of Jove: As if removed from man, the God of truth Had hid in desert plains his will divine. Alas! Otanes, that dread power which dwells Within these lonely walls, hath long received My fears and adorations; at his altars My gifts were offered, and my incense rose; But gifts and incense never can atone For crimes like mine: to-day I shall receive Answers from Memphis.

SCENE VI.

Sémiramis, Otanes, Mitranes.

Mitranes: An Egyptian priest Is at the palace gate, and begs admittance.

Sémiramis: Then will my woes be ended, or complete. Let us begone, and hide from Babylon Her queen's disgraceful sorrows: let Arsaces Be sent to me: soon may his presence calm This storm of grief, and soothe my troubled soul!

ACT II.

Arsaces, Azema

Azema: To thee, Arsaces, this great empire owes Its lustre, I my liberty and life. When vanquished Scythia, thirsting for revenge, From its wild desert rushed indignant forth, And bore down all before it; when my father, Oppressed by numbers, fell, and left me there A hapless slave; then, armed with thunder, thou, Piercing their dark retreats, didst break my chains, And give me ample vengeance on my foes. Thou wert my great deliverer, Arsaces, And in return I give thee all my heart; I will be thine, and only thine; but O! Our fatal passion will destroy us both: Thy generous heart, too open and sincere, Believed that gallant deeds, and fair renown In arms, would gain thee honors in a court; And, fearless of success, thou bringest with thee A hero's fierceness and a lover's heart. Assur is incensed: alas! thou dost not know him: He is too powerful for us; he rules all At Babylon; and much, I fear, abuses His fatal influence o'er Sémiramis: He is thy great inexorable–rival.

Arsaces: Ha! does he love thee?

Azema: No; that savage mind, Subtle and dark, a foe to every virtue, Insensible to love and every charm But those ambition boasts, could never feel A real passion for me: but he knows That Azema is descended from the race Of our Assyrian kings, and soon may claim My right of empire here, as next the throne; And therefore means to blend his interest here With mine, and gain the sceptre for himself: But if the youth whom Ninus had decreed, Even from my infant years, to be my husband, The son of great Sémiramis, and heir Of Babylon, were living now, and here Would offer me his heart and half his empire, By love I swear, and by thy precious self, Ninias should sue in vain, and see me quit A throne with him for banishment with thee. Even Scythia's bleak inhospitable plains Would yield a sweet asylum to our love; For they would echo my Arsaces' name, And sound his praise; those barren wilds, where first Our passion grew, would be to me a court, Nor should I cast a thought on Babylon. But much I fear this subtle statesman means To carry his resentment further still: I've searched his soul, and know the blackness of it: Or I mistake, or guilt sits lightly on him; Already he is jealous of thy glory, He fears, and hates thee.

Arsaces: And I hate him more, But fear him not, since Azema is mine: Keep thou thy faith, and I despise his anger. At least I share with him the royal favor: I saw the queen, and her humanity Equalled the pride of Assur: when I fell Prostrate before her, gently she upraised me, And called me the support of Babylon: With pride I heard the flattering voice of her Whose name contending kings unite to honor: The distance 'twixt her royal state and mine Was lessened soon by mildest condescension; It touched, it melted me; and, after thee, To me she seemed, of all the human race, Most nearly to resemble the divine.

Azema: If she protects us, Assur's threats are vain: I heed them not.

Arsaces: Inspired by thee, I went, Fearless and brave, to lay before the feet Of my great mistress, that aspiring passion Which Assur dreads, and Azema approves; When lo, that very moment came a priest From Egypt with Ammonian Jove's decree: Trembling she opened quick the awful scroll, First fixed her eyes on me, then sudden turned Her face aside, and wept: stood fixed in grief Like one distraught, then sighed, and vanished from me. They tell me, she is fallen into despair, And hath of late been dreadfully pursued By some avenging god: I pity her: 'Tis wonderful that after fifteen years, Heaven, that so long defended, should at last Oppress her thus: by what hath she offended The angry gods, and wherefore are they changed?

Azema: We hear of naught but dreadful spectres, omens, And vengeance from above: the queen of late Lets loose the reins of empire: we had cause To fear for Babylon, least subtle Assur, Who knows her weakness, in this dangerous time, Should seize the helm, and bury all in ruin; But the queen came, and all was calm again; All owned the power of her despotic sway. If I have any knowledge of the court, The queen hates Assur, but keeps fair with him, And watches close; they're fearful of each other, Would quarrel soon, but that some secret cause, Some mutual interest, still prevents a rupture: I saw her fire indignant at his name; The blushes on her cheeks betrayed her thoughts, And her heart seemed to glow with deep resentment: But sudden changes happen in a court; Return, and speak to her.

Arsaces: I will; but know not Whether again I e'er shall gain admittance.

Azema: Thou hast my vows, my wishes, and my prayers For thy success: I glory in my love, And in my duty: let Sémiramis Rule o'er the vanquished East, I envy her Nor fame nor conquest; let the world be hers, Arsaces mine: but Assur comes this way.

Arsaces: The traitor! how I shudder at his presence! My soul abhors him.

SCENE II.

Assur, Arsaces, Azema.

Assur: Your reception, sir, I find, was noble, such as kings have oft Solicited in vain: you saw the queen In secret, did she not reprove a conduct Injurious to my honor and her own? Did she not tell thee Azema's designed For Assur, not for thee? Long since her hand To Ninias given was for the blood of kings Alone reserved; and therefore is my right, As next to the throne: did she acquaint you, sir, Into what fatal snares your pride would lead you, That neither fame nor honors will excuse Your bold pretensions?

Arsaces: I well know what's due To your high birth, and to the rank you bear, And should have paid it, though you had not thus Instructed me; but as a master here I own you not: your royal ancestors, From Belus sprung, perhaps may give you claim To Azema; the welfare of the state, Present and future, all, I own, conspire To raise your hopes of bliss, and make her yours: These are your claims, and I acknowledge them: But I have one that's worth them all: I love her: I might have added this, that I avenged And saved her, gave new lustre to the throne Which she was born to fill, if I had chosen, Like thee, to boast of my exploits before her. But I must leave thee, to perform her orders. Sémiramis and her I shall obey, And them alone: a day perhaps may come When thou shalt be our master: heaven sometimes In anger sends us kings: but thou art deceived, At least in one of thy ambitious views, If amongst thy subjects thou hast ranked **Arsaces: Assur:** The measure's full: thou courtest thy own destruction.

SCENE III.

Assur, Azema.

Assur: I've borne his insolence too long already, 'Tis time we enter on a nobler subject, And worthier thy attention.

Azema: Can there be one? But speak.

Assur: Ere long all Asia shall attend On our resolves, and low concerns like these Must pass unheeded by: a world demands Our mutual care: Sémiramis is now The shadow of herself, her glory's past, That star which shone with such transcendent lustre, Declining now, sends forth a feeble ray; The people see and wonder at her fall, Whilst every tongue demands a—successor: That word sufficeth: you well know my right: 'Tis not for love to deal forth sovereign power, And point out who shall rule in Babylon; Not that my soul, to beauty blind, would make A virtue of insensibility; But I should blush for thee and for myself, To see the welfare of a nation thus Dependent on a sigh: thoughts worthier both Must guide my fortune, and determine thine: Our ancestors the same, we should offend Their venerable shades, and lose the world By not uniting: I astonish you: These are harsh words for tender age like thine; But I address me to the kings and heroes From whom you sprung, to all those demigods Whom here you represent: too long trod down Beneath a woman's feet their ashes lay, Their glories she eclipsed, usurped their power, And fettered vanquished nations with her laws; But she is gone, and thou must now support The building she had raised: she had thy beauty, And thou must have her courage: let not love Or folly wrest the sceptre from thy hand, But grasp it close: you will not sacrifice To a Sarmatian's idle passion for you The name you ought to honor, and the throne You should ascend, of universal empire.

Azema: Let not Arsaces be the theme, my lord, Of your reproaches, but depend on me To vindicate the honor of my race, And to defend, whene'er occasion calls, The rights of my loved ancestors; I know Their worth and virtues, but I know not one Amongst the heroes which Assyria boasts More great, more virtuous, more beloved, than he, Than this Sarmatian, whom you thus disdain. Do justice to his merit: for myself, When I shall bend to Hymen's laws, the queen Must guide my choice, and at her hands alone Will I receive a master: for the crowd, The babbling echo of one secret voice, I heed it not; nor know I if the people Are tired of their obedience to a woman, But still I see them bow the knee before her; And if they murmur, murmur in the dust: The hand of heaven, they say, is raised against her: I am a stranger to her guilt, but think That heaven would never have made choice of thee To tell its high commands, or minister

Its justice to mankind: Sémiramis Is still a queen, and you who lord it here Receive from her the laws which you dispense: For me, I own her power, and hers alone: My glory is to obey, be thine the same.

SCENE IV.

Assur, Cedar.

Assur: Obey! I blush to think how long already I have obeyed: O insupportable! But say, hast thou succeeded, are the seeds Of hatred sown in secret through the realm? Will they spring up into a fruitful harvest Of discord, and rebellion?

Cedar: All is well: The people, long deluded by the arts And dazzling glory of Sémiramis, At length have lost their idle veneration: No longer chained to silence, they demand A successor: each lover of his country Calls for a master, and looks up to thee.

Assur: Heart-burning care! and ever-during shame! Still must my hopes, my fate depend on her? Was it for this that Ninus and his son Fell by my hand, that Assur might be still Only her first of slaves? So near the throne, To languish in illustrious servitude, And only be the second of mankind! The queen was satisfied with Ninus' death, But I went further, and pursued my blow: Ninias, in secret murdered by my order, Opened my passage to the throne; but she Denied me entrance.—A long time in vain I soothed her pride with flattery on her charms; Still hoped one day to gain upon her youth That happy influence which assiduous care And humble adoration seldom fail To win o'er artless minds that bend with ease: I little knew the firmness of her soul, Inflexible, and bold; the world alone Could satisfy her pride: she seemed indeed Most worthy of it: spite of my resentment, I own she was, and yield the praise she merits. The reins of empire, that flowed loose before, Strongly she held; appeased the murmuring crowd, Silenced their plaints, and quashed conspiring rebels; Fought like a hero, like a monarch ruled: She led her army and her people captive, And spite of fame, with more than magic art, Chained down the minds of men: the universe Astonished stood, and trembled at her feet. In short, her beauty, woman's best support, Strengthened the laws which power and valor made; And when I strove to raise conspiracies My friends stood mute, and only could admire her. At length the charm is broke: her power decays; Her genius droops;

remorse, and idle fears, And fond credulity have bound her faith To lying oracles, which knavish priests Had taught to speak in Egypt's barren plain: She pours her daily incense at their altars, And wearies heaven with vows: Sémiramis Creeps on a level now with common mortals, And condescends to fear: I know her weakness: Know, till she falls, Assur can never rise: But I have raised the people's voice against her, And she must yield: this blow decides her fate: If she consents to give me Azema, She is no longer queen; if she refuses, The kingdom will revolt: on every side The snare is laid, and nothing now can save her. Yet, after all, perhaps I am deceived, And fortune, so long called for, comes at last But to betray me.

Cedar: If the queen is forced To name a successor, and yields the princess To Assur's bed, what can he have to fear, When the divided branch of Asia's kings Shall be united? all conspires to pave Your way to empire.

Assur: Azema is safe; She must be mine; but wherefore send so far For this Arsaces? she supports him too; And when I would chastise his insolence, Her interposing hand prevents me still: A minister without the power, a prince Without a subject, girt around with honors, And yet a poor dependent, what is Assur? All, all unite to persecute me now: A peevish mistress, and a haughty rival, Consulted priests that teach their gods to speak Against me; with Sémiramis, who strives To free herself, yet trembles at my presence: But we shall see how far this proud ingrate Will urge an angry rebel who defies her.

SCENE V.

Assur, Otanes, Cedar.

Otanes: My lord, the queen commands you to attend her In secret, and alone.

Assur: I shall obey Her sacred orders, and with care perform My sovereign's will.

SCENE VI.

Assur, Cedar.

Assur: Whence springs this sudden change? These three months past she has avoided me, Even as the object of her hatred: oft When she beheld me she would cast her eyes Down on the earth, as if she loathed the sight: Whene'er we met, 'twas in a gaping crowd Of hearers; when she spoke, her sighs and tears Would interrupt our converse, or perchance Silence was all the answer she would give me. What can she want? What can she say to me? But here she comes: 'tis she—wait you within. [To Cedar.]

SCENE VII.

Sémiramis, Assur.

Sémiramis: My lord, I come to ease a troubled heart Of its long hidden woes, and pour it all Before you: I have ruled o'er Asia long, And not ingloriously: Babylon perhaps May pay this tribute to my memory, And say Sémiramis deserved to rank Among the greatest of her kings: thy hands Have helped me to support the weight of empire; With absolute dominion have I ruled, Adored by all, and crowned with victory On every side: intoxicated long With flattery's pleasing incense, I forgot The crimes that raised me to this envied state; Forgot the justice of high heaven: it comes; It speaks to me: Sémiramis must yield: This noble structure, which I fondly thought Superior to the injuries of time, Is tottering now, and shakes from its foundation; Means must be found to strengthen and support it.

Assur: The work is yours, and you must finish it: Foresee the attacks of time, and stop his rapine: Who shall obscure the lustre of thy days, Or wherefore fearest thou heaven whilst earth obeys thee?

Sémiramis: Yonder the ashes of my husband lie; Canst thou look there, and wonder at my fears?

Assur: I cannot bear to hear the noisy crowd Still talk of Ninus: wherefore should remembrance Call back the thoughts of that inglorious reign? Can they believe, that, after fifteen years, His angry spirit still calls out for justice? Ere now he would have taken due vengeance on us, Had he the power: why from the peaceful realms Of dark oblivion wouldst thou call the dead, Or search for truth in lying oracles? I am astonished too, but 'tis at thee, And thy vain fears: to make the gods propitious, We must be resolute: this idle phantom, At once the child and parent of your fears, Why should it thus alarm you? Prodigies Never appear to those who dread them not: Baits to allure the unthinking multitude, By knaves invented, and by fools believed; The great despise them: but if nobler views Inspire thy soul to immortalize the blood Of Belus, if the beauteous Azema Claims her high rank.—

Sémiramis: Assur, on that I came To speak with thee: our Babylon demands, For such is Ammon's will, a successor: Heaven and my people will be satisfied When I shall take a partner to my throne: Thou knowest, my pride could never condescend To a divided sway; 'twas my resolve To rule alone, while the impatient world Urged me in vain; and when the people's voice, Which now is echoed by the voice of heaven, Still presses me, in the bloom of youth, to give A sovereign to mankind, I still refused: If I had yielded then to any claim, It had been thine; you had a right to hope, And to expect it; but you knew too well, How much Sémiramis abhorred a master. Without submitting to a tie so fatal, I made thee then the second of mankind, And only not my equal; 'twas enough, I thought, to satisfy even thy ambition. At length the gods make known their will divine, And I obey them: hear the oracle: "All shall again be well at Babylon, When Hymen's torch a second time shall blaze Propitious; then shalt thou, O cruel wife, And wretched mother, then shall thou appease The shade of Ninus." Thus the voice of heaven Declares its sacred will: I know thy arts; Know, thou hast formed a party in the state, And mean to oppose me with the royal blood From whence you sprung: from thee and Azema My successor, it seems, must rise; I know You look that way, and she perhaps aspires To equal honors; but, observe me well: I shall not suffer your united claims To rob me of my right: remember, sir, You know my will; 'tis constant, and as fate Irrevocable: thinkest thou now the God Whose arm is lifted o'er me hath deprived My soul of all its wonted strength and spirit, Or dost thou still behold Sémiramis, Who can support the honor of her throne? Know, Babylon ere long shall at my hands Receive a master: whether the high choice Shall fall on thee, or be another's lot, I'll take a sovereign as a sovereign ought: Bring me the magi and the princess here To join their voices with Sémiramis. To give away my freedom and my empire Is the first, greatest act of royal power, And therefore let it be performed with awe And silence due to my authority. Heaven hath appointed this great day to show Its mercy to me, and the gods at length Remit their anger; nothing can disarm it But my repentance; 'tis the only virtue: Trust me, it is, howe'er you may despise it, Remaining for the guilty: weak, I know, And fearful thou esteemest me; but henceforth Remember, Assur, guilt alone is weakness: Think not that fear can e'er disgrace a throne, It has done good to kings, and might to thee; I tell thee, statesman, to obey the gods, And tremble at their power, is no abasement.

SCENE VIII.

Assur: [Alone.] Astonishment! such language, such designs! Or is it artifice, or weakness in her, Or cowardice or courage? Does she mean, By yielding thus, to prop her tottering power, And by our union to defeat my purpose? I must not think, it seems, of Azema, Because, perhaps, I'm destined for herself. It must be so. What all my cares in vain Solicited, my flattery of her charms, My deep intrigues, and our united crimes, With all her fears, could never gain, at length An idle dream, and a dark oracle From Egypt have performed. What power unknown Decrees the fate of mortals? Great events Hang on the slenderest thread: still I am doubtful: I'll see Sémiramis again; she seemed Too much in haste; such sudden resolutions Betray an overanxious mind, and those Who change with ease are either weak, or wicked.

ACT III.

Sémiramis, **Otanes**: [The scene represents an apartment in the palace.]

Sémiramis: Who would have thought, Otanes, that the gods, Offended as they were, at length should smile Propitious thus, and threaten but to save! Should drop the uplifted thunder from their hand, And pardon me; should send Arsaces hither To change my fate! for know it is their will That I should wed, and by a second tie Expiate the crimes of my first fatal nuptials. They are the great disposers of our hearts, And mine with pleasure yields to their decrees: It even outruns their purposes: Arsaces, I'm thine; for thou wert born to rule o'er me, And o'er the world.

Otanes: Arsaces! he!

Sémiramis: Thou knowest, In Scythia's plains, when I avenged the Persian, And conquered Asia, this young hero fought Beneath his father's banners, and, surrounded With captives, brought to me the bloody spoils, And, blushing, laid his victims at my feet. When first I saw him, I could feel his heart, As by some secret power, attracting mine Insensibly towards him; all mankind, Besides Arsaces, seemed not worth my notice. Assur grew jealous of him, and ever since Has fired with indignation at his name; Whilst his dear image still employed my thoughts, Before that voice which guides my every word And every action named him for my husband, Before the gods had pointed out Arsaces Otanes. It was indeed a noble conquest, thus To bend that haughty spirit which disdained The proffered homage of our Eastern monarchs, Who as her subjects, not as lovers, still Accepted kings! You who contemned those charms, That sovereign beauty, which extended wide Your universal empire; whilst your eyes Pierced every heart, you scarce would condescend To mark their power; and dost thou yield at last To love's imperious sway; to fears and horror Succeed the tender passions? Can it be?

Sémiramis: O, no; it is not love: I am not fallen So much beneath myself, as to bestow On beauty the reward that's due to virtue; I feel a nobler passion in my breast: Alas! such weakness would but ill become Sémiramis: unhappy as I am, For me to think of love, Otanes, how Couldst thou suppose it? Once I was a mother, But scarce had studied to deserve the name By my fond cares, when heaven in anger snatched My child away, and left me here alone A prey to anguish. I had nothing near me That I could love; and, midst my grandeur, felt An aching void within my soul. I fled The court, endeavored to avoid myself, And sought relief in these proud monuments, Amusing flatterers of a restless heart That shunned reflection: rest was still a stranger, And long remained so; but he comes once more, I feel him now, and wonder at the power That charmed him hither: 'twas Arsaces; he Shall hold the place of husband and of son, A conquered world, and all my glories past. How much I owe to thee, celestial power, Who thus propitious leadest me to the altar So long abhorred; and hast thyself inspired That passion which alone can make me happy!

Otanes: But what will be the rage and grief of Assur? Hast thou reflected on it, when he hears Thy new resolves? He is not without hopes: The people have already fixed thy choice On him, and his resentment will not end In mere complaints.

Sémiramis: I never have deceived, And therefore fear him not: these fifteen years, Whate'er his views have been, I've taught him still To rank but with my subjects, though the first Amongst them; and set bounds to his ambition, Which he hath never o'erleaped: I reigned alone; And if this feeble hand so long could guide The helm of power, and curb his haughtiness, What can his courage or his cunning do Against Arsaces and Sémiramis? Yes: Ninus hath accepted my repentance, And leaves the mansions of the dead to urge Our happy union: his illustrious shade Again would rage to see his murderer seize His throne and bed: this calls him from the tomb, And Ammon's oracles unite with him To crown my bliss: no more the awful virtue Of Oroes affrights me; I've sent for him To be a witness of the great event, And soon expect him here.

Otanes: His honored name And sacred character may give indeed A sanction to your choice.

Sémiramis: I know it will, And establish my resolves.

Otanes: Behold, he comes.

SCENE II.

Sémiramis, Oroes,

Sémiramis: Great successor of Zoroaster, welcome: To-day must Babylon receive a king; Thy office is to crown him; is all ready For the solemnity?

Oroes: The magi wait Thy pleasure, and the nobles all attend: To pay obedience to the sovereign power Is all my duty, and I shall fulfil it: I am not to judge kings, for that belongs To heaven alone.

Sémiramis: By this mysterious language, It seems you disapprove my purpose.

Oroes: Madam, I know it not, but wish it fair success.

Sémiramis: Thou canst interpret heaven's high will: these signs Which I have seen, can they be fatal to me? A spectre hath of late, perhaps some god, Appeared, and in the bosom of the earth Re-entered soon: what power hath thus broke down The eternal barrier that divides the light From darkness? wherefore should a mortal thus Rise from the tomb to visit me?

Oroes: Know, heaven Doth oft suspend its own eternal laws When justice bids, reversing death's decree; Thus to chastise the sovereigns of the earth, And terrify mankind.

Sémiramis: The oracles Demand a sacrifice.

Oroes: It shall be offered.

Sémiramis: Eternal justice, thou whose piercing eye Beholdest my naked heart, O fill it not Again with horror, bury in oblivion My first unhappy nuptials! Oroes, stay. [To Oroes, who is retiring.]

Oroes: [Returning.] I thought my presence might disturb you, madam.

Sémiramis: Return, and answer me: this morning, say, Did not Arsaces offer at your altars Gifts to the gods?

Oroes: He did; and precious were they: Arsaces is the favorite of heaven.

Sémiramis: I know he is, and I rejoice to hear it. Can I be wretched if I trust to him?

Oroes: He is the empire's best support; the gods Conducted him; his glory is their care.

Sémiramis: With transport I accept the fair presage, Whilst hope and peace return to calm my breast. Away: again let purest incense rise Before your altars; let your magi come And sanctify the choice; bring down the smiles Of the assenting gods, and make us happy. Henceforth may Babylon with me revive, And shine amongst the nations of the earth With double splendor! Go thou, and prepare The solemn pomp.

SCENE III.

Sémiramis, Otanes.

Sémiramis: Heaven seconds my design, And I am only the interpreter Of its high will, to give the world a master: Thus to receive a kingdom at my hand Will strike him with astonishment: even now How little thinks he of the approaching greatness! How will proud Assur and his fawning crowd Be humbled! But a word, and the whole earth Falls at his feet; and, grateful as he is, I know he will repay me: I shall wed him, And for my portion carry him a world; My glory's pure, and now I shall enjoy it.

SCENE IV.

Sémiramis, Otanes, Mitranes. An Officer of the Palace.

Otanes: Arsaces begs admittance to your presence, To lay his sorrows at your feet.

Sémiramis: Arsaces! What sorrows can Arsaces feel when I Am near him, he who thus hath banished mine? Quick, let him come: he knows not yet his power O'er the fond heart of his Sémiramis. O thou dread shade whose voice alarmed my soul, Whose blood no more calls out for vengeance on me, And you, the guardian gods of this great empire. Of the Assyrians, Ninus, and my son, Unite to bless Arsaces! Ha! the sight Alarms me; whence can these strange terrors rise?

SCENE V.

Sémiramis, Arsaces.

Arsaces: O queen, I am devoted to thy service; My life is thine; and when I shed this blood, I am rewarded if it flows for thee. My father had some small renown in arms; I saw him perish bravely in the field, And at the head of thy victorious bands; He left his hapless son a fair example, Perhaps but ill pursued: I'll not recall The memory of my father's services. 'Twould ill become me; at your royal knees, Though here I sue for favor and protection: Pity the rashness of a guilty youth, Who listened to the dictates of imprudence. And even in serving feared he might offend you.

Sémiramis: Offend me! thou, Arsaces! fear it not.

Arsaces: To-day you give your kingdom and your hand: My heart, I know, should on the great event Keep secret all its fears, and humbly still In silence, with depending monarchs, wait To know our master; but this Assur steps So haughtily, and triumphs in his conquest, We cannot brook his pride: the people call him Already their new sovereign; his high blood And rank support him: may he prove himself Worthy of both! but I have still a soul Too proud to bend beneath him, or adore The power I had defied: his jealous heart I know detests Arsaces: let me then Retire in safety, far from him, and thee: Permit me to revisit the dear climes Where first I served my royal mistress, there His tyranny can never reach: perhaps I may hereafter—

Sémiramis: Wilt thou leave me then, And fearest thou Assur?

Arsaces: No: Arsaces fears Naught but the anger of Sémiramis. Perhaps thou knowest my fond ambition, then I've cause indeed to tremble.

Sémiramis: Hope the best, And know that Assur ne'er shall be thy master.

Arsaces: I own it shocked my soul to look on him As Ninus' successor: but is he then Designed for Azema? forgive this bold Presumptuous questioner: long since I know She was to Ninias given, proud Assur sprung From the same race, and claims her as his own: I am but a poor subject, yet I dare—

Sémiramis: Such subjects are my kingdom's best support; I know thee well; thy noble soul, superior To vulgar minds, hath sought Sémiramis, Not for her fortunes, but herself; thy eyes Are fixed on her true interest, and on thee I shall depend: Assur and Azema Shall never meet; their union would be dangerous: But their designs are known, and by my care Will be prevented.

Arsaces: Since my heart at length Is open to thee, and thou hast discovered—

Azema: [Enters suddenly, and throws herself at the feet of Sémiramis.] O queen, permit me thus—

Sémiramis: Rise, Azema: Where'er my choice may light, thou mayest depend On my protection, and shalt find respect Due to thy birth; for, destined as thou wert To be the wife of my lamented son, I look upon thee with a mother's eye: [To them both.] Go, place yourselves with those whom I have called To witness my resolves, and mark my choice. [To Arsaces.] Be thou, my best protector, near the throne.

SCENE VI.

The apartment of Sémiramis opens into a magnificent saloon richly ornamented; a number of officers in their proper habits on the steps of the throne, which is raised in the middle; the satraps on each side: the high priest enters with the magi, and places himself between Assur and Arsaces: the queen in the midst with Azema, and her attendants: guards at the lower end of the saloon.

Oroes: Ye princes, magi, warriors, the support Of Babylon, assembled by command From great Sémiramis, the will of heaven Soon shall ye know: the gods that guard our empire Have fixed on this important hour to work A great and mighty change; whoe'er the queen Shall here appoint her sovereign and our own It is our duty to obey; and here I bring my tribute to the throne, my prayers And wishes for the glory and the welfare Of them, and of their kingdom: may these days Of joy and gladness ne'er be changed to hours Of grief and sorrow, nor these songs of mirth To mournful plaints!

Azema: A king, my lords, will soon Be named; whoe'er he be, the choice will injure Myself alone; but Azema was born And must remain a subject; I submit To the queen's pleasure, and on her protection Shall still depend; nor with the dark presage Of future ills shall interrupt your joy: But leave you my example of obedience.

Assur: Howe'er the queen may choose, and heaven determine, We must consult the public good alone; Let us then swear by this imperial throne, And great Sémiramis, to yield submissive, And without murmuring to obey her will.

Arsaces: I swear it; and this arm that fought for her, This heart obedient ever to her voice, Which next the voice of heaven I still revered, This blood which flowed with pleasure for her sake, Shall be devoted to that royal master Whom she appoints.

High Priest: I wait the great award Of heaven and **Sémiramis**: **Sémiramis**: Enough: Each to his place, and now attend, my people. [She seats herself on the throne. Azema, Assur, Oroes (the high priest) and Arsaces take their places, and she proceeds.] If in that hand which custom and the laws Of an imperious husband had confined To homely cares, and to a distaff chained, I bore aloft the sceptre and the sword, Beyond my subjects' hope, nor sunk beneath The weight of empire, let me now extend To latest times its glory: 'tis my purpose This day to take a partner in the throne: The gods must be obeyed, whose dread command At length subdued my long unconquered heart: They who deprived me of my son, perhaps May one day raise an heir to Babylon Worthy of empire, who shall follow me Through all the thorny paths that I have trod, Finish my work, and make my reign immortal. I might have chosen a sovereign from the kings That dwell around me, but they are all my foes, Or tributary slaves: a foreign hand Shall never wield this sceptre: my own subjects Are better than the kings which they have conquered: Belus was born a subject; if he gained The diadem, he owed it to the people, And to himself: by rights like his I hold The power supreme; and, mistress of a kingdom Larger than his, have bent beneath my yoke The nations of the East, which Belus ne'er Had seen or heard of: what he but attempted Sémiramis performed; for they who found A kingdom, and they only, can preserve it. You want a king who may be worthy of you, Worthy of such an empire, shall I add Worthy the hand that crowns him, and the heart Which I shall give: I have consulted heaven, My country's weal, the interest of mankind, And choose a king to make the world more happy. Adore the hero, see in him revived The princes of my honored race; observe him, And know, this king, this hero, is—Arsaces. [She descends from the throne, and they all rise.]

Azema: Arsaces! the perfidious—

Assur: Rage and vengeance!

Arsaces: Believe me, Azema—

Oroes: Just heaven! avert These omens.

Sémiramis: Thou who sanctifiest my choice, Confirm it at the altar: see in him Ninus and Ninias both restored. [It thunders, and the tomb shakes.] O heaven! What do I hear?

Oroes: Great gods, protect us now!

Sémiramis: The thunder comes, in anger or in love I know not: pardon, gracious gods! Arsaces Must win them to forgiveness. Ha! what voice Distracts me thus? and see, the tomb is open. O heaven! I die. [The ghost of Ninus comes out of the tomb.]

Assur: The shade of Ninus' self. Gods! is it possible?

Arsaces: What sayest thou? speak, Thou god of terrors.

Assur: O unfold thy tale.

Sémiramis: Comest thou to pardon, or to punish me? It is thy sceptre and thy bed which here I have bestowed: speak, is he worthy of it? Determine: I obey thee.

The Ghost of Ninus: [To Arsaces.] Thou shalt reign, Arsaces, but there are some dreadful crimes Which thou must expiate: hie thee to the tomb, And to my ashes offer sacrifice: Serve me and Ninias: remember well Thy father: listen to the pontiff.

Arsaces: O! Thou venerable shade, thou demigod, Who dwellest within these walls, the sight of thee Inspires but does not amaze Arsaces: Yes, I will go, on peril of my life, And meet thee in the tomb: but tell me, what Must be the sacrifice? O speak! he's gone. [The ghost retires towards the entrance of the mausoleum.]

Sémiramis: Thou honored spirit of my lord, permit me Thus on my knees to pour my sorrows forth, Permit me in the tomb to—

Ghost: [At the entrance of the tomb.] Stop: no farther: Respect my ashes: when the time is come I'll send for thee. [The ghost goes into the tomb, and the mausoleum closes.]

Assur: Amazing!

Sémiramis: Follow me, My people, to the temple: be not thus Dismayed: for know, the gentle shade of Ninus Is not implacable; it loves your king, And therefore will it spare Sémiramis: Heaven that inspired my choice will now support it: Haste then, and pray for me, and for Arsaces.

ACT IV.

SCENE I.

Representing the porch of the temple.

Arsaces, Azema.

Arsaces: Do not oppress me in this hour of grief, And aggravate my sorrows; I have borne Enough already: this dread oracle Affrights me; prodigies on every side Disturb the course of nature: heaven deprives me Of all, if Azema is lost.

Azema: No more, False man, nor to the horrors of this day Add the remembrance of thy perfidy; No more the terrors of Sémiramis, The walking spectre, and the opening grave, Appal me now; of all the prodigies Which I have seen, thy base inconstancy Hath shocked me most: go on, appease the shade Of Ninus, and begin the sacrifice With Azema; behold, and strike the victim.

Arsaces: It is too much; my heart was not prepared Against this cruel stroke: thou knowest, my soul Prefers thee to the empire of the world: What was the object of that fame in arms I held so dear, of all my victories? All my ambition hoped for was at last To merit thee: Sémiramis, thou knowest, Was dear to both; thy tongue unites with mine To praise her; she was still the guardian god That cherished and protected us; as such We both revered her with that pious zeal And chaste regard which mortals bear to heaven: Judge of my spotless faith by my surprise At the queen's choice, and mark the precipice It leads us to, thence learn our future fate.

Azema: I know it.

Arsaces: Learn, that neither thou nor empire Were destined for Arsaces; know, that son Whom I must serve, the child of Ninus, he Who must inherit here—

Azema: Well; what of him?

Arsaces: That Ninias, he who from his cradle lit The torch of Hymen with thee, who was born My rival and my master—

Azema: Ninias!

Arsaces: Lives; And will be with us soon.

Azema: Ha! then the queen—

Arsaces: Even to this day deceived, laments his death.

Azema: Ninias alive!

Arsaces: It is a secret yet Within the temple, and she knows it not.

Azema: But Ninus crowns thee, and his widow's thine.

Arsaces: Ay, but his son was born for Azema; He is my king, so says the oracle, And I must serve him.

Azema: But love claims his own, And will be heard in spite of all, Arsaces: His orders are not doubtful, or obscure. Love is my oracle, and that alone Shall be obeyed. Ninias, thou sayest, yet lives, Let him appear, and let Sémiramis Recall her plighted faith to him; let Ninus Rise from the tomb, to join the fatal knot Made in our infant years; let Ninias come, My king, thy master, and thy rival, fired With all the love which once Arsaces had For Azema, then see how I will slight His proffered vows; then shalt thou see me scorn The sceptre at my feet, and spurn a crown Which is my due: where is he now? What secret, What mystery veils him from us? Let him come; But know, nor Ninias, nor Sémiramis, No, nor the sacred spirit of his father Risen from the tomb, nor all the powers of nature Thrown in confusion, from my heart would wrest The image of my perjured dear Arsaces: Go, ask thy own, if it will dare to act As mine hath done. What are those dreadful crimes Which thou must expiate? if thou e'er shouldst break The sacred tie that binds us, if thou art false, I know no crime, no treachery like thy own. I see the sage interpreter of fate This way advancing, love will never plead Thy cause with heaven, if thou betrayest me: go, From Ninus' hand receive thy doom; remember, Thy fate depends on heaven, and mine on thee. [Exit **Azema**: **Arsaces**: Arsaces still is thine: stay, cruel maid:] How mingled is our happiness and woe! What strange events that contradict each other—

SCENE II.

Arsaces, Oroes, the Magi Attending.

Oroes: [To Arsaces.] Let us retire to yonder lonely walk; I see you are much moved: prepare yourself For strokes more dreadful. [To the magi.] Bring the royal wreath. [The magi bring the coffer.] This letter, and this sacred sword, to thee, Arsaces, I deliver.

Arsaces: Reverend father, Wilt thou not save me from the precipice That gapes before me? wilt thou not at length Uplift the veil, that from my eyes conceals My future fate?

Oroes: 'Twill be removed, my son; The hour is come, when in his dreary mansions, Ninus from thee expects a sacrifice That shall appease his angry spirit.

Arsaces: What Can Ninus ask, what sacrifice from me? Must I be his avenger, when his son Still lives? Let Ninias come; he is my king, And I will serve him.

Oroes: 'Tis his father's will, Thou must obey him: an hour hence, Arsaces, Be at his tomb, armed with this sacred sword, And with this wreath adorned, which Ninus wore, And which thyself did bring to me.

Arsaces: The wreath Of Ninus!

Oroes: 'Tis his royal will that thus Thou shouldst appear, to offer up the blood That must be shed; the victim will be there: Strike thou, and leave the rest to him, and heaven.

Arsaces: If he requires my life, I'll give it him: But where is Ninias? thou speakest naught of him: Thou hast not told me how his father gives To me his kingdom and his queen.

Oroes: To thee His queen! O heaven, to thee Sémiramis Be given! Arsaces, the important hour Which I had promised thee is come, when thou Shalt know thy fate, and this abandoned woman.

Arsaces: Great gods!

Oroes: 'Twas she who murdered Ninus.

Arsaces: She, Saidst thou, the queen?

Oroes: Assur, that foul disgrace Of human nature, Assur gave the poison.

Arsaces: I'm not surprised at Assur's cruelty, But that a wife, a queen, and such a queen, The pride of sovereigns, the delight of nations, That she should e'er be guilty of a crime So horrible! it passes all belief. How can such virtues and such guilt as hers Subsist together!

Oroes: How indeed! the question Is worthy of thy noble heart: but now 'Twere needless to dissemble, every moment Is big with some new secret, horrible To nature, who already whispers to thee Her soft complaints; thy generous heart, I see, Spite of thyself, is shocked, and mourns within thee: But wonder not that Ninus from the tomb Indignant rises on this seat of guilt; He comes to break the horrid nuptial tie, Woven by the furies, and expose to light Unpunished crimes; to save his son from incest: He speaks to, he expects thee: know thy father, For thou art Ninias, and the queen's thy mother.

Arsaces: Thou hast o'erpowered me in one dreadful moment With such repeated wonders, that I stand Astonished, and the night of death surrounds me. Am I his son, and can it be?

Oroes: Thou art: Ninus, the morn before he died, foresaw His end approaching; knew the deadly draught Which he had drunk was ministered to thee By the same hand, and, dying as thou wert, Withdrew thee from this wicked court: for Assur Had poisoned thee that he might wed thy mother, Thought to exterminate the royal race, And open thus his passage to the throne: But whilst the kingdom mourned thy loss, Phradates, Our faithful friend, secreted and preserved thee; With skilful hand the precious herbs prepared, O'er Persia spread by her benignant God, Whose wondrous power drew forth the latent venom From thy parched limbs: his own son dying, you Supplied his place, and still wert called Arsaces. He waited patient for some lucky change, But the great judge of kings had otherwise Determined; truth at length descends from heaven, And vengeance rises from the tomb.

Arsaces: O God! Enough already hast thou tried thy servant, Or must I yield that life which you restored? Yes: I was born midst grandeur, shame, and horror: My mother—Ninus! O what deadly purpose— But if the traitor Assur was alone To blame, if he—

Oroes: [Giving him the letter.] Behold this paper here, Too faithful witness of her guilt, then say If yet a doubt remains.

Arsaces: Haste, give it me, And clear them all. [He reads.] Ha! "Ninus to Phradates: I die by poison, guard my Ninias well, Defend him from his foes: my guilty wife—"

Oroes: Needest thou more proof? this witness came from thee. He had not finished; death, thou seest, broke off The imperfect scroll, and stopped his feeble hand; Phradates hath unfolded all the rest, Read this, and learn the whole. [Gives him another paper.] It is enough That Ninus hath commanded thee, he guides Thy steps, and leads thee to the throne, but says He must have blood.

Arsaces: [After reading the paper.] O day of miracles, And you, ye dreadful oracles from hell, Dark as the tomb which I must visit, how Shall I unveil your secret purposes, When he who is to make the sacrifice Knows not his victim! Who shall guide my choice? I tremble at it.

Oroes: Tremble for the guilty. Amidst the horrors that oppress thy soul, The gods will guide thee; deem not thou thyself A common mortal, from the race of men Thou art distinguished, set apart by heaven, And noted by its signature divine, Walk thou secure, though night conceals thy fate, The gods of thy great ancestors employ thee But as their instrument. What right hast thou To litigate their power, and to oppose Thy masters? Saved from death, as thou hast been, Be thankful still; complain not, but adore.

SCENE III.

Arsaces, Mitranes.

Arsaces: I cannot reconcile this strange event: Sémiramis my mother! can it be?

Mitranes: [Entering in haste.] My lord, the people in this hour of terror Demand their king: permit me first to hail thee The husband of Sémiramis, and lord Of Babylon: the queen is hasting hither In search of thee; I bless the happy hour That gave her to thee: ha! not answer me! Despair is in thy looks, thy lips are closed In dreadful silence, thou art pale with terror, And thy whole frame's disordered: what has passed? What have they said?

Arsaces: I'll fly to **Azema**: **Mitranes**: Amazing! can it be Arsaces? fly A queen's embraces; scorn her proffered love; Insult her choice; the royal hand that spurned Kings for thy sake! thus are her hopes betrayed?

Arsaces: Gods! 'tis Sémiramis herself; O Ninus, Now let thy tomb in its dark bosom hide Her crimes, and me!

SCENE IV.

Sémiramis, Arsaces.

Sémiramis: Arsaces, all is ready, We want but thee, great master of the world, Whose fate, like mine, depends on thee; O haste, And make our bliss complete! with joy I see Thy brows encircled with that sacred wreath: The priest, I know, was by the gods commanded To crown thee with it; heaven and hell at once Approve my choice, and by these signs confirm it: Assur's seditious party, struck with awe And holy reverence, tremble at my presence; Ninus, at length propitious, hath required A sacrifice, O haste, and give it him, That we may soon be blest: the people's hearts Are all with us, and Assur's threats are vain.

Arsaces: [Walking about with great emotion.] Assur! away! in his perfidious blood The parricide—we will revenge thee, Ninus.

Sémiramis: What do I hear? just heaven! speakest thou of him, Of Ninus?

Arsaces: [Wildly.] Saidst thou not, his guilty hand [Coming to himself.] Had shed—to arm against his queen! the slave, That was enough to make me hate him.

Sémiramis: Haste then, Receive my hand, and thus begin thy vengeance.

Arsaces: My father!

Sémiramis: Ha! what looks are those, Arsaces? Is this the soft submissive tender heart Which I expected from thee, when I gave My willing hand? That fearful prodigies, And spectres rising from their dark domain, Should leave the marks of horror on thy soul, Alarms me not, I feel them too, but less When I behold Arsaces: do not thus O'erspread this fairest dawn of happiness With sorrow's gloomy shade, but still appear Such as thou wert when trembling at my feet, Lest Assur e'er should be thy master; fear Nor him, nor Ninus and his angry shade; My dear Arsaces, thou art my support, My lord, my husband.

Arsaces: [Turning aside from her.] 'Tis too much, O stop: Her guilt o'erwhelms me.

Sémiramis: How his soul's disturbed! Alas! he wants that peace which he bestowed On me.

Arsaces: Sémiramis—

Sémiramis: What wouldst thou? speak.

Arsaces: I cannot: leave me, leave me: hence! begone.

Sémiramis: Amazing! leave thee! can I e'er forsake Arsaces? O explain this mystery to me, And ease my tortured soul: it makes us both Unhappy:—ha! despair is in thy aspect; Thou chillest my veins with horror, and thy eyes Are dreadful; they affright me more than heaven And hell united to oppose my vows: Scarce can my trembling lips pronounce, I love thee: Some power invisible now leads me on Towards thee, now withholds me from thy arms, And mingles, how I know not, tenderest love With sentiments of horror and despair.

Arsaces: Hate me, abhor me.

Sémiramis: Canst thou bid me hate thee? Cruel Arsaces, no: I still must trace Thy footsteps, still my heart must follow thine: What is that paper which thou lookest on thus With horror, whilst thy eyes are bathed in tears, Does that contain a reason for thy coldness?

Arsaces: It does.

Sémiramis: Then give it me.

Arsaces: I must not: darest thou—

Sémiramis: I'll have it.

Arsaces: Leave to me that dreadful scroll, To thee 'twere fatal, I have use for it.

Sémiramis: Whence came it?

Arsaces: From the gods.

Sémiramis: And wrote by whom?

Arsaces: Wrote by my father.

Sémiramis: Ha! what sayest thou?

Arsaces: Tremble.

Sémiramis: Give it me, let me know at once my fate.

Arsaces: Urge it no more; there is death in every line.

Sémiramis: No matter: clear my doubts, or I shall think That thou art guilty.

Arsaces: Ye immortal powers That guide our steps, it is to your decrees That I submit.

Sémiramis: For the last time, Arsaces, I here command thee, listen, and obey.

Arsaces: [Giving her the letter.] O may thy justice, heaven, be satisfied! And this the only punishment that e'er Shall be inflicted on her! now 'tis past, And thou wilt know too much. [She reads.]

Sémiramis: [To Otanes.] What do I read? Support me, or I die. [She faints.]

Arsaces: She sees it all.

Sémiramis: [Coming to herself, after a long silence.] Delay not, but fulfil thy destiny: Punish this guilty, this unhappy wretch, And in my blood wash out the deadly stain. Nature deceived is horrible to both, Avenge thy father, strike, and punish me.

Arsaces: No: let the sacred character I bear, The name of son, preserve me from that crime! Much rather would I pierce the heart of him Who still reveres thee, the poor lost **Arsaces: Sémiramis:** [Kneeling.] Be cruel as Sémiramis; she felt No pity, therefore be the son of Ninus, And take my life: thou wilt not; nay, thy tears Even mix with mine: O Ninias, 'tis a day Of horrors, yet there's pleasure in this pain. Before thou givest me what I have deserved, The stroke of death, let nature's voice be heard: O let a guilty mother's tears bedew That dear, that fatal hand.

Arsaces: I am thy son, 'Tis not for thee, whate'er thy guilt, to fall Thus at my feet: O rise, thy Ninias begs, He loves thee still, still vows obedience to thee, Respect and purest love: consider me As a new subject, only more submissive, More humble, than the rest; I hope, more dear. Heaven that restores thy son is sure appeased: The gods who pardon thee reserve their vengeance For Assur; leave him to his fate.

Sémiramis: Receive My crown and sceptre, I have much disgraced them.

Arsaces: Still, I beseech you, hold me ignorant Of all, and let me with the world adore you.

Sémiramis: O no: my guilt's too flagrant.

Arsaces: But repentance May blot it out.

Sémiramis: Ninus hath given to thee The reins of empire, thou must not offend His vengeful spirit.

Arsaces: O it will relent At thy remorse, and soften at my tears. Otanes, in the name of heaven, preserve My mother, and conceal the horrid secret.

ACT V.

SCENE I.

Sémiramis, Otanes.

Otanes: O 'twas some god that smiled propitious on thee, Who thus prevented these abhorred nuptials; Whilst nature shuddered at the approaching danger, Gave thee a son, and saved thee thus from incest. The oracles of Ammon, and the voice From hell, the shades of Ninus, all declared The day appointed for thy second marriage Should end thy sorrows, but they never said That marriage e'er should be accomplished: No: The nuptials were prepared: thou hast fulfilled Thy destiny: thy son reveres thee still: Mild is the justice of offended heaven, Which only asks a private sacrifice: This day Sémiramis shall still be happy.

Sémiramis: Alas! there is no happiness for me, Otanes: Ninias smiles indeed upon me: A mother's sorrows for a time will plead More strongly with him than the blood of Ninus, And my past crimes; but soon his tenderness And filial love may change perhaps to wrath And fierce resentment for a murdered father.

Otanes: What fearest thou from a son? what dire presage—

Sémiramis: Fear is the natural punishment of guilt, And still attends it: this detested Assur, Has he attempted aught, say, does he know What passed of late, and who Arsaces is?

Otanes: The dreadful secret still remains unknown; The shade of Ninus is by all revered; But how to comprehend the oracle They know not; how they must avenge his ashes; How serve his son—the minds of men are struck With wild astonishment, in silence now They wait the hour when the self-opened tomb Shall banish all their fears, and make them happy. Meantime the soldiers are in arms, the people Crowd to the altars; wretched Azema, Trembling and pale, with terror in her looks, Walks round the tomb, and lifts her hands to heaven; Whilst Ninias stands astonished in the temple, Prepared to strike his victim yet unknown: The gloomy Assur meditates revenge, Unites the remnants of his scattered party, And forms some dark design.

Sémiramis: I have kept fair Too long already with him: seize the traitor, Otanes, bear him to my son in chains; Ninias shall soon appease eternal justice, At least with Assur's blood, my vile accomplice. Ninus, thou seest I am a mother still; Thou seest my heart, O take it, take it all, And may it rise a grateful sacrifice! Ha! who approaches with such hasty steps? How everything appals my fluttering soul!

SCENE II.

Sémiramis, Azema, Otanes.

Azema: O Queen, forgive me if I come uncalled; But terrors worse than death have forced me thus To clasp thy knees, and beg thy royal mercy—

Sémiramis: What wouldst thou, princéss? speak.

Azema: To snatch a hero From instant danger, stop a traitor's hand, And save **Arsaces: Sémiramis:** Ha! what hand? Arsaces!

Azema: He is thy husband, Azema's betrayed, He lives for you alone; no matter—

Sémiramis: He My husband! gods!

Azema: The sacred tie that binds you—

Sémiramis: The tie is dreadful, impious, and abhorred: Arsaces is—but speak, go on; I tremble: What dangers? haste, and tell me.

Azema: Well thou knowest, Perhaps this very moment, whilst I ask Thy aid, perhaps—

Sémiramis: Well, what?

Azema: That demigod Whom we adore, demands the sacrifice Within the dreary labyrinths of the tomb: What are the crimes Arsaces must atone for I know not.

Sémiramis: Crimes! just heaven!

Azema: But impious Assur Hath sworn to violate that sacred place Which mortals dare not enter.

Sémiramis: Ay! indeed! Hath Assur sworn it?

Azema: In the dead of night The wily traitor had long since secured A safe retreat, if e'er occasion called, Within the secret windings of the tomb, Where now he means to do the bloody deed, To brave the powers of hell, and wrath of heaven; With sacrilegious hand he would destroy The generous **Arsaces**:
Sémiramis: Heaven! what sayest thou? By what detested means?

Azema: Believe a heart By love enlightened, and by love inspired: I know the traitor's rank envenomed hatred, Marked how the trembling faction by his zeal Revived; I pried into their secret councils, Pretended to unite his cause with mine, And join our interests; I have looked into him, Have wrested from his heart the fatal secret. Boldly he marches on, and hopes to pass Unpunished: well he knows that none dare enter That holy place, not Oroes himself: Thither he's gone: meantime his slaves report Arsaces is the victim that must die For Babylon, and Ninus in his blood Shall satiate his revenge: the nobles meet, The people murmur; Ninus, Assur, heaven, Are all incensed: I tremble for **Arsaces**:
Sémiramis: My dearest Azema, heaven speaks by thee: It is enough: I see what must be done. Repose thyself with safety on a mother; Daughter, our danger is the same; go thou, Defend thy husband, I will save my son.

Azema: O heaven!

Sémiramis: I meant to wed him, but the gods In mercy have forbade it: they inspire A hapless mother now—but time is precious; Go: leave me here, and in my name command The nobles, priests, and people, to attend me. [Azema goes into the porch of the temple, and Sémiramis advances toward the tomb.] Thou shade of Ninus, lo! I fly to avenge thee; The hour is come when thou didst promise me Admittance to thy tomb; I have obeyed thee, Called by thy voice, behold me here to save My son. Ye guards that wait around my throne Approach: henceforth Arsaces is your king; No more obedient to Sémiramis, Observe his laws, to him the sovereign power I here resign: be you his subject now, And his defenders. [Guards appear, and range themselves on each side at the further part of the stage.] Gracious heaven! protect me. [She goes into the tomb.]

SCENE III.

Azema: [Returning from the porch of the temple to the front of the stage.] What can she purpose? O it is too late To save him now; I know not what to think: 'Tis wondrous all; O 'tis a dreadful moment, Arsaces! Ninias! ye immortal powers Who guide our fate, O say, did you restore My loved Arsaces but to snatch him from me?

SCENE IV.

Azema, Ninias.

Azema: Ha! Ninias! can it be? Art thou indeed Great Ninus' son, my sovereign, and my husband?

Ninias: O! thou beholdest me, Azema, ashamed To know myself, sprung from the blood of gods, And shuddering at the thought: O! Azema, Remove my terrors, calm my troubled soul, Strengthen my arm upraised to avenge a father.

Azema: Take heed how thou performest that dreadful office.

Ninias: He hath commanded, and I must obey.

Azema: Ninus would never sacrifice his son: Impossible!

Ninias: What says my Azema?

Azema: Ne'er shalt thou enter that abhorred place, For know, a traitor lies in wait for thee.

Ninias: Who shall withhold or terrify Arsaces?

Azema: Thou art the victim to be offered there: With sacrilegious steps the impious Assur Profanes the sacred tomb, and rashly dares To violate its privilege divine: He waits thee there.

Ninias: Good heaven! then all is plain; I'm satisfied: the victim is prepared; My father, poisoned by the wicked Assur, Demands the traitor's blood: instructed thus By Oroes, and conducted by the gods, Armed by the hand of Ninus' self, I go To punish the assassin: thither led By heaven's eternal justice, my weak hand Is but the instrument of power divine: The gods do all, and my astonished soul Yields to that voice which must decree my fate: Spite of ourselves, our ways are noted down, Marked, and determined: prodigies are spread Around the throne, and spirits called from hell To wander here: but fearless I obey. Believe, and trust in heaven.

Azema: Whate'er the gods Have done but fills my soul with sad dismay: Ninus was loved by them; yet Ninus perished.

Ninias: But now they will avenge him: cease thy plaints.

Azema: Oft have they chose the purest victim, oft Have shed the blood of innocence.

Ninias: No more; They will defend whom thus they have united: They by a father's voice exhorted us, Gave me a throne, a mother, and a wife. Soon shalt thou see me sprinkled with the blood Of the vile murderer; from the tomb those gods Shall lead me to the altar; I obey; It is enough: the rest be left to heaven.

SCENE V.

Azema: [Alone.] O guard his footsteps in this fatal tomb! Ye powers inscrutable, whose blood must flow This day? I tremble for the event, and dread The hand of Assur, long inured to slaughter; Even on his father's ashes may he shed The blood of Ninias: O may the dark womb Of hell receive and swallow up his rage! Ye lightnings blast him! O illustrious shade Of Ninus, wherefore wouldst thou not permit A wretched wife to go with her dear lord? O guide, support him in this place of darkness! Did I not hear the voice of Ninias mixed With deadly groans? O would this sacred tomb, Which I profane, but open to my wishes The gate of death!—I will descend:—I go— Hark! the earth shakes, and dreadful lightnings flash Athwart the skies: fear, hope, despair—he comes.

SCENE VI.

Ninias, a Bloody Sword in His Hand, Azema.

Ninias: O heaven! Where am I?

Azema: O! my lord, you're pale, And bloody, frozen with horror.

Ninias: 'Tis the blood Of the vile parricide: I wandered down Even to the bottom of the tomb; my father Still led me onward through its winding paths, He walked before, and pointed out the place Of my revenge: there, by the imperfect light That glimmered through the dreary vault, I saw, Or thought I saw, upraised the murderer's sword: Methought he trembled; guilt is ever fearful: Twice did I plunge my sword into his heart, And with my bloody arm, which rage had strengthened, Had dragged him in the dust towards the place Whence the dim rays of light appeared: and yet I own to thee, his deep heart-rending sighs, The mournful sounds, imperfect as they were, That reached my ears, his humble vows to heaven, With that repentance which in his last hour Seemed to possess his soul, the hallowed place, The voice of pity, which, revenge once o'er, Calls loudly on us, with I know not what Of dark mysterious terror, shook my soul, And made me leave the bleeding victim there. What can this trouble, this strange horror mean That dwells upon me, Azema? My heart Is pure, ye gods, my hands are innocent, Stained only with the blood you bid me shed; I've served the cause of heaven, and yet am wretched.

Azema: The dead are satisfied, and nature too: Come let us quit this horrid place, and seek Thy mother, she shall calm thy troubled mind: Since Assur is no more—

SCENE VII.

Ninias, Azema,

Assur: [Assur appears at a distance with Otanes, surrounded by guards.]
Azema: O heaven! he's there.

Ninias: Assur!

Azema: O haste, ye ministers of heaven, Ye servants of the king, defend your master.

SCENE VIII.

Oroes, the High Priest, with the Magi and People Assembled, Otanes, Ninias, Azema, Mitranes, Assur. [Disarmed.]

Otanes: They need not: by the queen's command I've seized The traitor, who attempted to profane Yon sacred monument, and enter there: I shall deliver him to thee.

Ninias: Alas! What victim then hath Ninias sacrificed?

Oroes: Heaven is appeased, and vengeance now complete. Behold, ye people, your king's murderer. [Pointing to Assur.] Behold, ye people, your king's successor. [Pointing to Ninias.] 'Tis Ninias, Babylon's lost prince, restored: He is your sovereign, know him, and obey.

Assur: Thou Ninias!

Oroes: Ay; 'tis he: the guardian god, Who saved him from thy rage, hath brought him hither; That god whose vengeance hath o'erthrown thee.

Assur: Ha! did Sémiramis then give thee life?

Ninias: She did, and power withal to punish thee: Guards take him hence, and rid me of a monster. He was not worthy of my sword; to fall By Ninias' hand had been a death too glorious. The victim hath escaped me; let him die, Even as he lived, with infamy: away.

Assur: It is my heaviest punishment to see Ninias my sovereign: but 'tis pleasure still To leave thee more unhappy than myself; [Sémiramis appears at the foot of the tomb, wounded, and almost dead, one of the magi supporting her.] Look yonder, and behold what thou hast done. [Pointing to Sémiramis: Ninias.] Whom have I slain?

Azema: Fly, my dear Ninias, fly This fatal place.

Mitranes: What hast thou done?

Oroes: [Placing himself between Ninias and the tomb.] Away; And cleanse those bloody hands: give me the sword, That fatal instrument of wrath divine.

Ninias: No: let me plunge it to my heart. [He attempts to destroy himself, the guards interpose.]

Oroes: Disarm him.

Sémiramis: [Brought forward and seated on a sofa.] Revenge me, O my son; some base assassin Has slain thy mother.

Ninias: O unhappy hour; Unheard of guilt! for know, that base assassin, That monster was—thy son: this hand hath pierced The breast that nourished and supported me: But soon thou shalt have vengeance, Ninias soon Shall follow thee.

Sémiramis: I went into the tomb To save thee, Ninias; thy unhappy mother— But from thy hands, I have received the fate I merited.

Ninias: This last, this fatal stroke, Sinks deep into my soul: but here I call Those gods to witness who conducted me, Those who misled my steps—

Sémiramis: No more, my son: Freely I pardon thee, and only make This last request, that those dear hands may close My dying eyes. [He kneels.] A mother begs it of thee: Thy heart I know was stranger to the deed: O would that I had been as innocent When Ninus died! but I have suffered for it. Henceforth let mortals know, that there are crimes Offended heaven never can forgive. O Ninias, Azema, let your blessed union Blot out my crimes; come near your dying mother; Give me your hands; long may ye live and reign In happiness! that hope still gives me comfort, And mingles joy even with the pangs of death. It comes, I feel it. O! my children, think On your Sémiramis, O do not hate My memory,—O my son, my son—'tis past.

Oroes: Her eyes are sunk in darkness: help the king And guard his life. Learn from her sad example, That heaven is witness to our secret crimes: The higher is the criminal, remember, The gods inflict the greater punishment; Kings, tremble on your thrones, and fear their justice.

End